WELCOME TO YOUR GENDER/SEXUALITY JOURNAL

(keep me in a safe place)

Copyright © 2023 Tyra Blizzard

All rights reserved.

ISBN: 978-1-7389517-1-0

CONTENTS

INTRODUCTION

Sexuality and gender are often studied and explored separately; however, there is tremendous magic in examining them side by side. The moment we shift our perspective to view gender beyond the binary, it becomes nearly impossible to analyze sexuality without applying a similar lens.

> For example, a straight woman is said to be attracted to men. But… What exactly is a man? What is a woman? Once we begin to question the constructs we have been socialized to accept, everything seems to fall apart.

Humans often require structure & patterns to feel safe and in control. The creation of boxes, labels, and categories makes it easier for us to conceptualize our complex world. However, for those of us who seek to escape from those boxes, we are either praised and revered or ridiculed and ostracized. Therefore, making sense of your gender identity and sexuality can be frustrating, & frightening.

It is essential to note that many of us do not have a safe space to openly question the uncompromising standards of heteronormativity & the gender binary. It is difficult to escape from boxes that are continually being taped down and reinforced.

This journal will guide you through the process of identity exploration by prompting you to reflect upon the conflicting concepts of gender & sexuality.

***

Reminder: Whether or not you can safely and openly express your authentic truth, nothing can stop you from exploring yourself in the privacy of your thoughts.

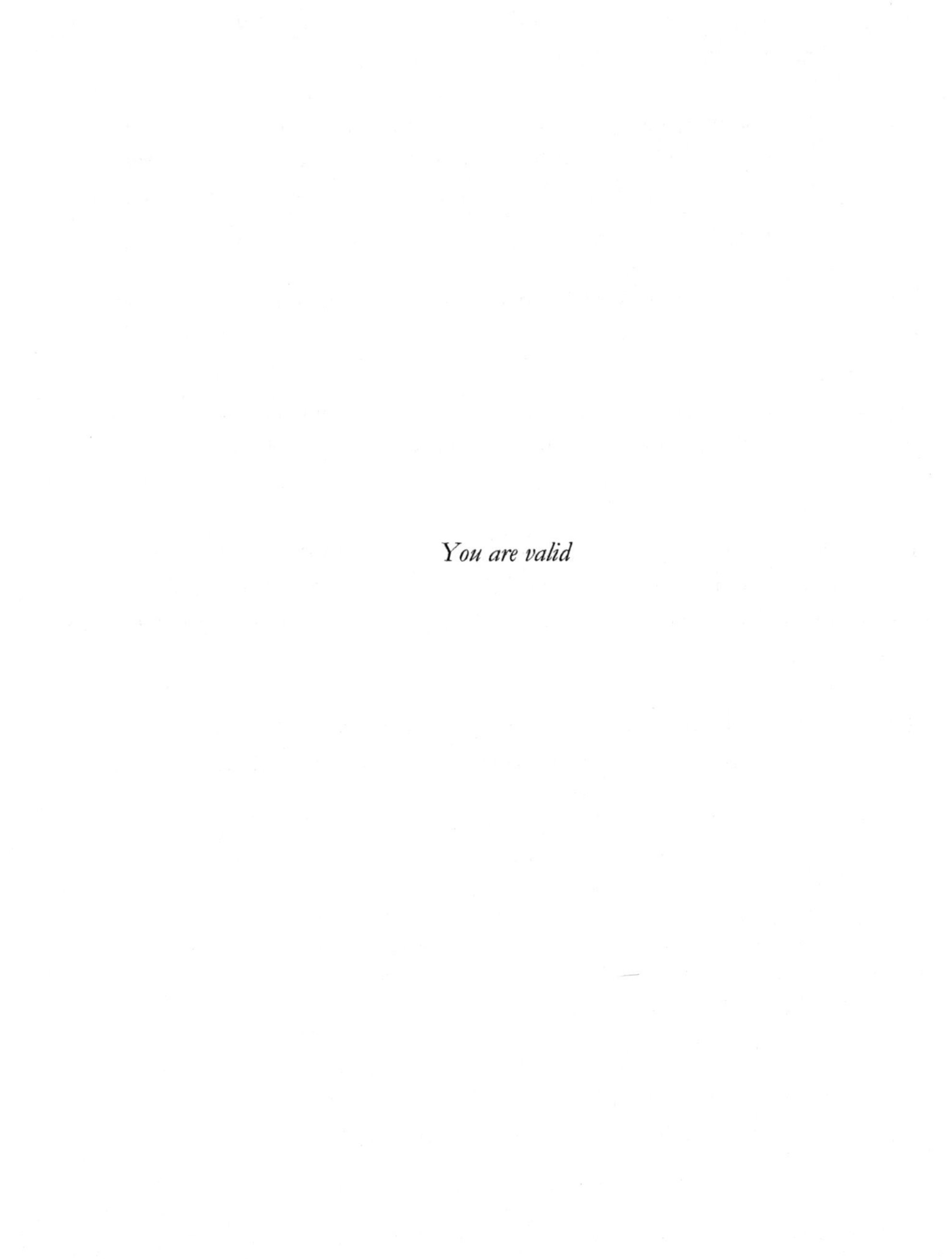

You are valid

A LETTER FROM THE AUTHOR

Hi, I'm Tyra.

You may not know me personally but, by the time you get through this journal, we'll likely have some things in common.

I spent 22 years of my life confidently identifying as a straight woman. Three years later, writing out that last sentence feels strange & uncomfortable because I've since fallen deep into an abyss of sociological mysteries, complexities & nuances. I transitioned from Cisgender Heterosexual Woman to Genderqueer Lesbian in what feels like the blink of an eye.

Gen•der•queer \jen-dər-kwir\

> "a vibe", a genderless entity that encompasses all the genders but also no gender, all at the same time- *that's how I define it at least.*

I often reflect on my past & giggle at my younger self who was so innocently ignorant of my impending gender/sexuality crisis. My favourite question as a child was, *why?* I would scrunch my eyebrows, lift my index finger & purse my lips in preparation to ask "why" as many times as I could until I could no longer find anyone to indulge my never-ending questions. I'm sure you can imagine how much fun that was for my parents.

My gender/sexuality crisis had been inching toward the edge of a precipice for so long; merely the subtle breath released upon saying the word *why* mustered up enough wind to blow down the tower of socialized rules & expectations I had spent my entire life building & reinforcing. Everything came to a violent crash, leaving nothing but a pile of sparkling rainbow ashes. As I rummaged through the debris, I realized none of the materials used to build this tower even belonged to me.

I asked myself, "who am I… & why?".

The younger version of me would have responded, "My name is Tyra Blizzard & I am a basketball player, a sister, a daughter, & I am a woman". The first three parts of my identity were relatively easy to understand. I am a basketball player because I play basketball. Simple enough, right? I am a sister because I have a brother. I am a daughter because I have parents. I am a woman because…

Um…

I am a woman because women are…

Hm…

What *is* a woman?

I have been a basketball player for the last 13 years. I believed wholeheartedly that basketball was the most significant part of my identity. #BallisLife, you know? I took that phrase way too literally. Anyway, my worth as a human being depended upon my success or failure as an athlete. As I matured & developed a healthier relationship with my sport, I learned to separate basketball from the core of my essence. I carried this mindset to Morocco, North Africa, as I prepared for the first year of my professional basketball career.

Living in a foreign country & not being able to communicate easily with the surrounding people can cause you to spend *a lot* of time by yourself.

Consistently existing in the confines of a gym or my tiny Moroccan apartment provided me with the perfect level of isolation necessary to embark upon my journey of gender & sexuality exploration. I shifted my perspective to see the world from a bird's-eye view. I could see myself more clearly because I was no longer engulfed in the noise, stimulation, & pressures of the world's insidious social constructs.

As I sat alone in my room, stewing in confusing thoughts about my identity & self-concept, I became hyper-aware of one of the most frustrating things about being a non-male athlete:

People remind us of the fact that we are not men… like, <u>all</u> the time.

I couldn't tell you the number of times I heard, "you're just a girl, I could probably beat you 1v1", from the middle-school boys I used to coach in basketball camps. I am a 25-year-old professional athlete & hundreds of 12-year-old boys confidently believe they could beat me playing basketball one on one. I could go on a thousand-page rant about misogyny in sports, but the point is, my perceived gender has always been at the forefront of my life experiences. Whether those experiences were positive or negative, everyone seemed to remind me I was a "woman". So, I believed it.

I had spent most of my life feeling comfortable identifying as a woman, yet I hadn't the slightest idea what being a woman meant to me.

> I am, however, a **Black** Woman.
>
> How can I be both Genderqueer & a Black Woman, you may ask? The answer is actually quite simple:
>
> I will always be a Black Woman because of how I am perceived by the people in the world around me & how those external perceptions shape my reality. Being a Black Woman also connects to my cultural and spiritual identity. My gender identity, however, is a mystery.

So, the question remains. What is a woman? What does it mean to be a woman? How can you define "womanhood" in a way that applies to *all* women?

This is when the deep dive began. I had spent years researching the human body from a biological & physiological perspective, so I figured I should start there.

I reflected upon all the information I had learned throughout elementary school, high school, and my university Human Kinetics degree (BHK).

In elementary school, I learned that boys have "pee-pees", and girls have "flowers". People still seem to define men & women similarly:

Man = Penis or Male Sex Characteristics
Women = Vagina or Female Sex Characteristics

I thought to myself,

> So… you can't identify as a woman if you don't have breasts, a vagina, or a uterus? Regarding both Cis & Trans women, not all women have breasts. Not all women have a uterus. What about intersex people? What about people who biologically do not fit the typical binary

concepts of male or female bodies? How do they fit into the gender binary?

The math ain't mathin'.

I ruminated on all the material I had learned in my biology, physiology, & sociology classes. It didn't take me long to recognize that any definition of "man" or "woman" that is based solely on biological or physiological characteristics is inaccurate (& often trans-exclusionary). Also… it just feels wrong to define people by their genitals.

Although the terms "sex" & "gender" are regularly used interchangeably, they are **not** the same.

Simply put: Sex = Biology & Gender = Sociology

Two different sciences folks.

Gender has absolutely nothing to do with biology because it is a social/colonial construct. Aka… humans made it up & just went along with it.

Thus began my research into the sociology & psychology of gender. I meticulously explored the social rules & norms associated with men, women, masculinity, and femininity.

I express both "feminine" and "masculine" characteristics but often feel limited by the rules associated with traditional femininity and womanhood. After exploring Gender Schema Theory; more specifically relating to psychologist Sandra Bem & the Bem Sex Role Inventory (1974); I began to seriously question my gender.

I had been socialized to perform the socially acceptable conceptions of my assumed gender & expected to incorporate those notions into my self-concept.

As I continued to delve into the mysteries of gender, I inevitably began questioning my sexuality. As a presumed straight woman, I never thought to question my attraction to men. Once again, one simple "why" was enough to blow away the cloak of heteronormativity that was dressed upon me the moment I entered this world. In my mind, I was the perfect straight woman. I was performing straightness in the exact way I had observed in my environment.

I exclusively dated tall football players who fit the mould of the stereotypical muscular hyper-masculine man.
But… What is a man?

What aspects of men & manhood am I attracted to? Am I *actually* attracted to men, or was I just socialized to believe I was?

Every piece of literature and media I was exposed to centred a heteronormative standard & storyline.

A man and a woman fall in love and live happily ever after.

I had never questioned the possibility that my happily ever after could be with a woman or a non-binary person.

I rushed to Google and typed, "am I gay?". I watched hours of YouTube videos, listened to numerous podcasts & read article after article yet, nothing seemed to portray exactly how I was feeling. My sexuality transitioned from straight, to bicurious, to pansexual, until I came across the infamous Lesbian Masterdoc & learned about compulsory heterosexuality.

The Lesbian Masterdoc is a 31-page online document that serves as a guide to navigating the complexities of understanding your sexuality as a woman. Essentially, it helps you determine the answer to the question: Am I a lesbian?

The document defines compulsory heterosexuality as the socially enforced expectation that "straight" is the default. It is the theory that heterosexuality is the only normal and acceptable sexual orientation. Compulsory heterosexuality is built into us from the moment we are born into this world, and it can take an eternity to recognize & dismantle it.

I asked myself, "how much of me is *actually* me, & how much of me has been determined by society?"

I had nearly confirmed my lesbian sexuality after that. I took it upon myself to condense the Lesbian Masterdoc into a 113-question quiz & film a YouTube video to share my exciting revelations with the world. One year later, that video had amassed over 41K views and inspired hundreds of people to comment & share that they had also begun questioning themselves. I continued to explore my identity online via my TikTok platform & created a playlist titled *Gender Crisis*. This playlist documents the entirety of my gender/sexuality journey from the very beginning to the present day.

I can now proudly express my evolution into an openly queer person who is constantly exploring, analyzing & deconstructing the societal norms that had trained me to believe I was a straight woman. I cultivated an online community of nearly 1 million people who are just as hungry to dissect all the subtle ways in which we have been socialized to fit into carefully curated heteronormative, Eurocentric boxes.

My greatest frustration with my gender/sexuality journey was, I often felt alone. I didn't know many queer people in my personal life & I couldn't entirely relate to the queer people online who were sharing their stories. We all have vastly unique experiences, environments, and identities that shape our perceptions of ourselves & the world around us. No YouTube video or "Am I Gay" quiz could tell me exactly what my gender/sexuality was.

I wished I had some sort of detailed journal to help guide me through my self-exploration. I wished I had a safe place to write about all my confusions, traumas, frustrations, & emotions relating to gender, sexuality & dating.

Hence, the creation of: *The Gender/Sexuality Journal.*

I am sharing my story to reassure you that you are not alone. It isn't easy to question the world as you know it or to question yourself. Your journey may not look exactly like mine, but at least you'll know there are other people out there who are going through a very similar process of self-exploration.

If, upon the completion of this journal, you realize you exist much further outside of the binaries of gender and sexuality than you had initially thought…

WELCOME TO THE CLUB BESTIE.

I am proud of you,

Tyra Blizzard

Mini Glossary

Agender: Folks who don't identify with any gender

Androgyne: Folks whose gender falls in-between masculinity and femininity, but they don't identify with either of them

Aromantic: Folks who don't experience romantic attraction much, or at all. This is usually experienced on a spectrum, meaning how much romantic attraction folks can experience varies from person to person

Asexual: Folks who don't experience sexual attraction much, or at all. This is usually experienced on a spectrum, meaning how much sexual attraction folks can experience varies from person to person

Bigender: Folks who identify with two genders

Bisexual: Folks who are attracted to people of their own and other genders

Cis/Cisgender: Folks who identify with the sex assigned to them at birth

Demiromantic: Folks who don't experience romantic attraction until they've established an emotional bond with the person or people

Demisexial: Folks who don't experience sexual attraction until they've established an emotional bond with the person or people

Femme: An umbrella term to describe feminine gender identities, gender expressions, and sexualities that is not limited to women

Gay: Men, non-binary or gender non-conforming folks who are attracted to other men, non-binary, or gender non-conforming folks. Also used as an umbrella term to describe same-gender attraction, in general

Genderfluid: Folks whose gender identity or expression fluctuates over time. This can mean days, weeks, months or years

Intersex: Folks who have unique hormones, reproductive organs, genitalia, or chromosome combinations that fall outside the assigned categories of male and female

Lesbian: Women, non-binary or gender non-conforming folks who are attracted to other women, non-binary, or gender non-conforming folks

Non-Binary: Folks whose gender identity doesn't fall into the assigned categories of male or female, also known as the gender binary

Pansexual: Folks who experience attraction to people of any gender

Polygender: Folks who identify with more than one gender, or folks who pass through different gender identities over time

Queer: An umbrella term to describe unique gender identities, gender expressions, and same-gender attraction. This was a harmful word used against members of the 2SLGBTQ+ community but some folks have started using it again for themselves! Remember to think about the meaning and impact this word could have before using it

Questioning: Folks who are exploring whether they experience attraction to people of their gender, or if they identify with a different gender identity

Straight: Folks who are attracted to people who do not share their gender identity. This is usually when a woman is attracted to a man, or a man is attracted to a woman. P.S. Remember that gender identity is different from sexuality – for example, someone can identify as a straight trans girl, or straight trans guy

Trans/Transgender: Folks who identify with a different sex or gender than the one assigned to them at birth

Two-Spirit: An identity specific to Indigenous folks that encompass both masculinity and femininity. Two-Spirit identity comes with its own cultural roles, which can involve relationships with the land, water, spirituality, community, and more

***

Visit sexfluent.ca for more information about gender & sexuality

SEXUALITY

To see beyond the binaries of gender & sexuality, you must first look within them.

This topic is split into two sections:

Section 1: Socialized as a Girl/Woman
Section 2: Socialized as a Boy/Man

The questions in this part of the journal are directly centred around the basic standards of heteronormativity to help you dissect & dismantle them from the inside out.

Feel free to explore whichever section resonates most with you (& of course, you can try both!)

***

Try your best to detach from any past version of yourself (aka, any version beyond yesterday). Answer these questions based on how you feel in the present moment.

SECTION 1

Sexuality: Socialized as a Girl/Woman

***

Attraction & Dating

Hi! If you're here, other people likely expect you to be attracted to Boys/Men. Here are some questions to help you explore this attraction further. If you come across a question that doesn't resonate with you, skip it & move on to the next question.

What is your type? What type of men are you normally attracted to?

Do you find you are most attracted to masculine men or, men who are feminine or androgynous?

Describe the non-physical traits & characteristics of your ideal partner.

Do you think these characteristics are unique to men? Do you know of any women who express these characteristics?

Describe your ideal partner physically (feel free to draw a picture)

What are your dating standards?

Do you think your dating standards are realistic enough for a man to meet? Why or why not?

Do you think your dating standards are realistic enough for a woman to meet? Why or why not?

Do you like the idea of being with a man but get uncomfortable when a man approaches you? Why or why not?

Do you see yourself physically & romantically being with one person for the rest of your life? Why or why not?

If you would like to get married one day, do you see yourself marrying & spending the rest of your life with a man? Why or why not?

Has this ever happened to you?

→ You had a crush on a boy/man until you learned he liked you back. Suddenly, your crush disappeared. Write about it.

Do you find men physically attractive, but can't seem to connect with them emotionally? Write about it.

Do you find it difficult to distinguish between a friendship and a romantic connection with a man?

Are you often attracted to unattainable men, such as fictional characters, older men, or men in relationships? If so, why?

Are you often attracted to unattainable women, such as fictional characters, older women, or women in relationships? If so, why?

Do you ever wish you weren't attracted to men? Why or why not?

Describe your past romantic relationships with men. Were they profound or surface-level?

Do you find yourself only being attracted to the men your friends are attracted to?

Do you think your attraction to a man has ever been influenced by the opinions of the people around you?

Are you emotionally attracted to women?

Are you physically attracted to women?

Describe some barriers that may prevent you from exploring your sexuality (ex. family, religion, school/work environment, etc.)

Sex & Intimacy

This subsection comprises 7 questions & 20 blank pages of unprompted journaling space to allow you to explore your relationship with sex & intimacy.

Reminder: Conversations about sex are healthy, important & valid. They can also be intimidating & triggering. If you do not yet feel comfortable exploring this section, skip it and return to it when you feel ready.

The following section begins on page: 71.

Do you enjoy sex or intimacy with men? Why or why not?

Do you fantasize about sex or intimacy with men?

Do you fantasize about sex or intimacy with women?

Do you engage in sex or intimate acts with men to whom you feel emotionally connected? Why or why not?

Have you ever enjoyed the feeling of being desired by a man more than the feeling of being with a man?

Do you engage in sober sex or intimacy with men? Why or why not?

Has this ever happened to you?

→ You feel you could be emotionally attracted to women, but the thought of kissing, being intimate, or having sex with a woman doesn't appeal to you. Why? Write about it.

Time to Journal

Use the next 20 blank pages to continue to explore your relationship with sexuality & intimacy.

The next section begins on page 71.

SECTION 2

Socialized as a Boy/Man

***

Attraction & Dating

Hi! If you're here, other people likely expect you to be attracted to Girls/Women. Here are some questions to help you explore this attraction further. If you come across a question that doesn't resonate with you, skip it & move on to the next question.

What is your type? What type of women are you normally attracted to?

Do you find you are attracted to feminine women, or women who are masculine or androgynous?

Describe the non-physical traits & characteristics of you your ideal partner.

Do you think these characteristics are unique to women? Do you know of any men who express these characteristics?

Describe your ideal partner physically (feel free to draw a picture)

What are your dating standards?

Do you think your dating standards are realistic enough for a woman to meet? Why or why not?

Do you think your dating standards are realistic enough for a man to meet? Why or why not?

Do you like the idea of being with a woman but get uncomfortable when a woman approaches you? Why or why not?

Do you see yourself physically & romantically being with one person for the rest of your life? Why or why not?

If you would like to get married one day, do you see yourself marrying & spending the rest of your life with a woman? Why or why not?

Has this ever happened to you?

→ You had a crush on a girl/woman until you learned she liked you back. Suddenly, your crush disappeared. Write about it.

Do you find women physically attractive, but can't seem to connect with them emotionally? Write about it.

Do you find it difficult to distinguish between a friendship and a romantic connection with a woman?

Are you often attracted to unattainable women, such as fictional characters, older women, or women in relationships? If so, why?

Are you often attracted to unattainable men, such as fictional characters, older men, or men in relationships? If so, why?

Do you ever wish you weren't attracted to women? Why or why not?

Describe your past romantic relationships with women. Were they profound or surface-level?

Do you find yourself only being attracted to the women your friends are attracted to?

Do you think your attraction to a woman has ever been influenced by the opinions of the people around you?

Are you emotionally attracted to men?

Are you physically attracted to men?

Are you physically attracted to men?

Describe some barriers that may prevent you from further exploring your sexuality (ex. family, religion, school/work environment, etc.)

Sex & Intimacy

This subsection comprises 7 questions & 20 blank pages of unprompted journaling space to allow you to explore your relationship with sex & intimacy.

Reminder: Conversations about sex are healthy, important & valid. They can also be intimidating & triggering. If you do not yet feel comfortable exploring this section, skip it and return to it when you feel ready.

The following section begins on page: 121.

Do you enjoy sex or intimacy with women? Why or why not?

Do you fantasize about sex or intimacy with women?

Do you fantasize about sex or intimacy with men?

Do you engage in sex or intimacy with women to whom you feel emotionally connected? Why or why not?

Have you ever enjoyed the feeling of being desired by a woman more than the feeling of being with a woman?

Do you engage in sober sex or intimacy with women? Why or why not?

Has this ever happened to you?

→ You feel you could be emotionally attracted to men, but the thought of kissing, being intimate, or having sex with a man doesn't appeal to you. Why? Write about it.

Time to Journal

Use these next 20 blank pages to continue to explore your relationship with sexuality & intimacy.

The next section begins on page 121.

SECTION 3

GENDER

In the previous section of this journal, you were guided through some questions to help you unpack standards of heteronormativity & how they affect you.

Now, it's time to dive into the gender binary & question what it means to be a woman or a man altogether.

What is your definition of a girl or a woman?

What is your definition of a boy or a man?

If you identify as a woman, why?

If you identify as a man, why?

Define femininity in your own words. List as many characteristics as you can.

Define masculinity in your own words. List as many characteristics as you can.

Do you feel connected to femininity? How?

Do you feel connected to masculinity? How?

If you could decide your gender (psst, you can by the way), what would you choose & why? Feel free to consult the Mini Glossary to answer this question.

Write what you like about the gender you were assigned at birth.

Write what you dislike about the gender you were assigned at birth.

Has filling out your gender on a form ever upset you or caused you to pause and reflect? Why or why not?

Do you ever feel you would be more comfortable in your skin if you lived life as a different gender? Write about that.

Do you ever feel like the gender you were assigned at birth isn't your true gender? Why?

Do you find that you must make a conscious effort to present as the gender you were assigned at birth? Write about that.

Do you ever feel you might be both a man & a woman, or neither? Write about that.

Do you feel peer or societal pressure to behave &/or present like the gender you were assigned at birth, even though it doesn't appeal to you?

Do some parts of your physical anatomy (ex. vagina, penis, breasts) make you dislike your body? Why or why not?

PRONOUN DRESSING ROOM

Try on a new pronoun

Write about yourself in the third person using the pronouns other people commonly use to describe you. Talk about your favourite colour, your favourite food & what you like to do in your free time.

Here is an example:

I know this really cool girl, her name is Betty. Her favourite colour is green, her favourite food is sushi, and her favourite pastime is reading.

Now, rewrite the same sentence using different pronouns. Continue to rewrite the sentence until you've tried on a few different pronouns.

Here are a few pronoun examples: she/her, he/him, they/them, ze/zir.

Which pronouns feel good? Why?

Which pronouns don't feel good? Why?

What are some barriers or fears that may deter you from using different pronouns? Write about it.

Have you ever considered changing your name? Why or why not?

If you could choose a different name, what would it be?

If you could redesign yourself from scratch with no external influence, what would you look like? How would you describe your gender identity? What would your pronouns be? What would your name be?

Draw a picture of that version of yourself.

Time to Journal

Use the rest of these pages to continue to explore gender & how it may or may not apply to you

How much of you is actually you & how much of you was predetermined by society?

You are valid

Made in the USA
Las Vegas, NV
31 May 2023